DO NOT TAKE YOUR DRAGON TO THE PLAYGROUND

WRITTEN BY JULIE GASSMAN
ILLUSTRATED BY ANDY ELKERTON

All morning you've worked and given your best.
You wrote, you read, you did a maths test.

It's now time for playtime, your well-earned break.
But before you head out, **please** avoid this mistake . . .

DO **NOT** TAKE YOUR DRAGON TO THE PLAYGROUND!

The rules of the playground are hard for a beast.
He'll break the first one as soon as released.

He'll run down the corridors, **shout** to his friends.
He'll **bump** into the Head with his spikey rear end!

Once she's outside, your dragon just cries!
She can't reach the bars, no matter how hard she tries.

Her arms are too small and her tail's in the way.
She makes such a **fuss** that no-one can play!

Maybe he'll promise to keep his feet on the ground
and offer to push you around and around.

He'll start out slowly, but soon he will run.
Then the ride becomes more scary than fun.

SO DO **NOT** TAKE YOUR DRAGON TO THE PLAYGROUND!

You might consider a game of catch.
But footballs and dragons are **not** a good match.

You see, dragons just **love** these types of games.
And when dragons are excited, out come the **flames!**

I see what you're saying, I know what you mean.
Dragons at playtime could create a real scene!

But **my** dragon is clever. He can learn all the rules.
He'll listen to teachers when he's playing at school.

He'll be **patient** and **take turns.**

He'll **share** all the toys.

He'll be **respectful** and **kind** to all girls and boys.

I know he can do it! You just have to agree.
Please let my dragon come play with me!

In my mind, dragons are all fire and wings.
I didn't know they were interested in slides and swings.

But I believe everyone deserves his or her chance
to run and to climb, to chase and to dance.

So if your dragon's respectful, well then, I'll say . . .

OF COURSE YOUR DRAGON CAN JOIN IN AND PLAY!

ABOUT THE AUTHOR

The youngest in a family of nine children, Julie Gassman grew up in South Dakota, USA. After college, she swapped small-town life for the world of magazine publishing in New York City. She now lives in Minnesota, USA with her husband and their three children. Julie's favourite playtime activity was playing swing ball, a game that would be quite challenging for a dragon with short arms.

ABOUT THE ILLUSTRATOR

After 14 years as a graphic designer, Andy decided to go back to his illustrative roots as a children's book illustrator. Since 2002 he has produced work for picture books, educational books, advertising, and toy design. Andy has worked for clients all over the world. He currently lives in a small tourist town on the west coast of Scotland with his wife and three children.

Raintree is an imprint of Capstone Global Library Limited, a company incorporated in England and Wales having its registered office at 264 Banbury Road, Oxford, OX2 7DY – Registered company number: 6695582

www.raintree.co.uk
myorders@raintree.co.uk

Designed by Ashlee Suker
Printed and bound in India

ISBN 978 1 4747 6138 3
22 21 20 19 18
10 9 8 7 6 5 4 3 2 1

British Library Cataloguing in Publication Data
A full catalogue record for this book is available from the British Library.